SPIRIT AND SOUL

SPIRIT AND SOUL

J.M. Goodrich

SPIRIT AND SOUL

Spirit And Soul is a collection containing eleven 100-word micro-fiction stories as well as three short stories, each one 1000-5000 words each.

ABOUT THE AUTHOR

J.M. Goodrich is a native of Michigan's beautiful upper peninsula. She loves spending time outdoors as much as she can with her family when she's not reading or writing. She has been published in several different anthologies and novels of her own. She has written stories of romance, fantasy, and horror. In addition to her love of writing, she has a passion for music, and an obsession with The Beatles.

ALSO BY J.M. GOODRICH

Deadly Celebrations

Emily's Wish

Snowflakes & Heartaches

Undying Love

Coming Home

Love Me Right

Summer Nights

100 WORD MICRO-FICTION

THE SLIT-MOUTH WOMAN

As I left the bar I decided to cut through the alleyway. The chill of the night air was almost more than I could handle. When I reached the end of the long, dark alley, a woman appeared.

"Am I pretty?" She asked as she approached me.

"Yes," I answered truthfully.

She then removed the scarf she wore, revealing a large slit through her mouth. It reached ear to ear. She batted her eyes, asking me again. "Am I pretty?"

Frozen in fear, I couldn't move, even though everything in me wanted to run.

When she smiled, my heart stopped.

BLOOD LUST

Damian licked his lips, making sure to get every last drop of blood. Can't let any go to waste, not that he ever did. Running his tongue over the tips of his fangs, he felt euphoric.

As much as he loved the feeling drinking blood gave him, Damian loved the feeling of watching his victims die a slow death more. He killed for sport more than the need for survival.

Damian smiled as his victim twitched for the last time, their body pale and now still. Satisfied, he lowered his lips to his victim's neck, draining the body completely dry.

WINDS OF DESTRUCTION

Solana stood on the roof of her house as the tornado began to form in the middle of her street. As she moved her hands in slow circles in front of her, the storm grew.

People began to take notice and ran away in fear. Their screams filled Solana with joy. She threw her head back and laughed as the winds picked up, cars started rocking, and roofs lost their shingles. Solana moved her hands, directing the winds as the storm intensified. Houses now collapsed, crushing whoever was trapped within, making her smile. No one messes with a storm witch.

Welcoming Home Our Ancestors

The flame of a single candle flickers in the window. It will help guide the spirits of our ancestors home. Extra chairs are set around the hearth, and the altar filled with their favorite foods to welcome our unseen guests.

The spirits who either are lost or have no descendants to provide for them are not forgotten. Along the paths and roadside apples are buried for them. It's not much, but we can't leave them with nothing.

To avoid harmful spirits, many people wear costumes and masks to disguise themselves, as well as carving turnips to look like protective spirits.

SURROUNDED BY DEATH

I watched in silent horror as they devoured my friends, limb from limb. Their decaying bodies hunched over their victims. The entire scene made me sick to my stomach.

I never believed in zombies before, now I was running for my life from them. Everywhere you looked held death and chaos - people running, being chewed on, limbs torn from their body.

I tripped over a half eaten leg as I tried to escape. A group of zombies was closing in, their broken, rotten bodies making their way to me. Their jerky movements sent shivers up my spine.

This was my end.

A Wailing Woman's Yearning

All through the night Margot wanders, searching for two young souls.

She peers in each window as she passes, stopping only when she finds the brother and sister.

While everyone else sleeps, she snatches them from their beds. Down to the river they go, to finish Margot's plan.

Taking one frightened child in each hand, Margot holds them under the water's surface, waiting for their struggle to end.

"Finally!" She cries, as she hugs the two lifeless bodies close. "What was taken from me has been returned!"

She looks at each child in turn. "Welcome home, my babies. Mommy's here."

THE NOT-SO-LUCKY CHARM

Joan held the amulet in the palm of her hand. She closed her eyes, concentrating as she cast the spell. Once it was complete, she carefully placed the amulet into a small box.

The next morning she presented the box to Amy, a coworker who thought Joan to be her best friend. Amy loved it, immediately slipping the amulet around her neck, swearing never to take it off.

As weeks passed, Amy's health deteriorated. Joan watched in silent joy, thankful that the spell was working. As long as Amy wore the amulet, her life would continue to be drained away.

LUGHNASADH CELEBRATIONS

The scent of sandalwood filled the air as we gathered for Lughnasadh. The hot days of summer were finally ending. Fresh fruits were ripe for the picking and grains ready to be harvested.
We give thanks for the bounty, and set fresh loaves of bread on the altar as an offering.
Now was the time for the Tailteann Marriage choosing. Women lined up one by one, to stick their hand through the door, to be chosen by a man who wished to marry her. Meeting for the first time today, they hoped this wouldn't lead to the Hill of Separation.

A Vampire's Fun

Moving the last bit of dirt away, Lars grips the lid of the coffin. He pried it open and smiled as the rotten air reached his nose. The corpse lying inside is perfect.

Lars gathers the body and adds it to his growing pile. He looks them over, feeling a little sad at the lack of blood. A little midnight snack would have been nice.

Tired of the way vampires have been treated, Lars has decided it's time for revenge. All the graves have been emptied, the corpses set up all over town. He couldn't wait to hear the screams.

THE COMING OF SPRING

It was sundown on February 1st. Our coven has come together to celebrate the coming of Spring. The candles were lit, ploughs decorated, the priapic wands being made.

The next morning we strapped on our snow gear for some peaceful snow hiking, searching for signs of Spring. Seeds were only beginning to stir in the Earth, so we didn't expect to see too many signs. After the hike we began our feast, where spiced wines, edible seeds, cakes, scones were passed around. Our Coven's High Priestess proudly wore her Crown of Lights, symbolizing the Goddess's return to her Maiden aspect.

DEADLY SCRYING

Under the light of the full moon, Kya stood at the
edge of a small pond. Her mind blank and body
buzzing with lunar energy, she fixed her gaze into
the depths of the water.

She stared, searching for the answers to her burning
questions. At last she saw images moving about in
the moonlit water. She wrote down three words in
her journal-red, swirl, end.

Kya didn't see the swirling mist that crept up on her
as she pondered their meaning. Slowly the mist
surrounded her, choking her life away, as the pond
water turned red with her blood.

SHORT STORIES

I Am The Friendly Ghost
Dead Girls Don't Cry
Flames Of Revenge

I AM THE FRIENDLY GHOST

J.M. Goodrich

"Don't worry, you'll be okay. You're going to make it."

Those were the last words I heard as I was wheeled into the emergency room. They were nice words, soothing words.

But they were wrong, it wasn't okay. I wasn't okay.

I didn't make it.

I don't know what I expected the afterlife to be like, but I'm sure it wasn't this. Instead of standing in a pool of fire or in front of some pearly gates, I was standing in the bedroom of what appeared to be a small child. The bed was covered in flower and heart shaped pillows. There was a hanging basket filled with teddy bears in the corner, and a small table in the center of the room that held a miniature tea set. I would have loved a room like this when I was younger.

And alive.

A voice down the hall startled me. "Why don't you go play in your room for a while?" It sounded like the mother of whoever's room this was. "It's almost time for bed anyway."

Panicking, I ran around the small room looking for a place to hide. At the last second I slid behind the door, mainly because it was the only spot big enough for me to fit. The door opened with a bang and it bounced off the wall, moving through me as if I wasn't even there.

Through the half opened door I could hear the little girl's parents as they argued. I remembered a couple similar moments from my own childhood. Sighing, the girl set her doll down at the table and walked over to close the door.

I stood as straight as I could. As the lock clicked, the little girl slowly turned her head towards me. "Who are you?" She asked quietly, looking me in the eye.

Crap. I wasn't sure what to do now.

"I. . . uh," I cleared my throat. "Hi. I'm Amber," I knelt down and held out my hand. Stupid move, but hey, I was new at this whole being a ghost thing. She just raised her eyebrows at me, making me feel even more like a fool.

"Are you a ghost?" She asked. "I can see through you. You have no skin"

I decided that I would just be honest with this little girl, since she didn't seem freaked out by my existence. "I am," I admitted, holding out my arms. I hadn't had time to fully take all this in yet, so I barely noticed that I was in fact, see through. It was almost like looking through a light fog. It was strange.

Her eyes lit up. "Cool. I'm Chelsea. You can be my friend, if you want," she said, walking back towards the table in the center of her room. "Let's have a tea party."

I smiled to myself as I helped Chelsea set up her plastic plates with cookies she had stashed in a drawer. The tea set was pink, matching most of the decor in her room, and was filled with water. I never had a tea set like this as a child, so this was another new experience for me. At least it was a fun one.

CHAPTER

TWO

I was amazed how easy it was for Chelsea to accept the fact that a random ghost was in her room. Kids are more accepting than most adults though. I was also amazed to find out that even though I was dead and see through and all that, I could still manage to sit, as best I could, on the tiny chairs and pick up the food and drinks.

"So you're really not afraid of me?" I asked. "I mean, I am a ghost after all and we don't know each other, so I'm still considered a stranger." At least, I'm pretty sure we didn't. Like my body, my memory is hazy now. I couldn't really remember anything clearly about my life. That fact terrified me. I didn't want to forget what my life had been like.

"Nope," she said, hugging one of her teddy

bears close. "I like you. You seem nice. I want us to be friends." She looked into my eyes again, her own growing a little misty. "I don't have any real friends. Mommy and daddy won't let me have any. They yell a lot too," she added as she looked sadly towards the door. "Only at each other, but I hate it."

I felt sorry for Chelsea. This poor little girl, all she wants is to feel loved. I walked over to her and knelt down. "They may yell a lot, but I'm sure they love you so much. I mean, how could they not? You're their daughter, and so darn cute." I said, trying to make her smile. "And I absolutely will be your friend." I hugged her.

"You will?" She beamed. "My first friend!" Her excitement was contagious, making me laugh.

Just then her father burst through her door, and the mood instantly changed. "Chels, who are you talking to?" He demanded, eyes darting around the room.

"My new friend," she replied cheerfully, pointing in my direction. "She's right there. Say hi daddy."

Nervous, I stood motionless as her father scanned the room. He didn't seem to see me at all.

"There's no one here, Chels. Keep your voice down, and start getting ready for bed." He looked around the room one more time before closing the door.

"Why didn't daddy see you?" Chelsea asked me once he was gone. "You're right here. I see you."

"I'm not sure," I shrugged. "I'm just as confused as you are."

"Well, I see you. You're real. And you're my friend," she said through a yawn.

I turned away as she changed into her pajamas and then I helped tuck her into bed. I had a feeling no one else would be here to do it.

"Amber," she said as I was about to turn off the light. "Will you be here when I wake up?" She sounded so hopeful.

"Of course I will," I smiled. "We're friends, and I'll always be here for you."

Satisfied that she would no longer be alone, Chelsea snuggled deeper into her blankets and closed her eyes. I turned off the light and silently vowed to watch over this sweet little girl for as long as I could. She needed me. Even dead, I would always be her friend.

DEAD GIRLS DON'T CRY

J.M. Goodrich

Three best friends decide to get revenge on the girl who's been tormenting them for years.Secretly, they've been dabbling in witchcraft, drawn to its addictive and seductive power. Will their revenge be everything they hoped for, or will there be dire consequences?

THREE

"Hey Rose, do you still have that perfume I like? The one I borrowed last time I was over?" Lana asked.

She could hear objects being moved around through the speaker phone. They always spoke to each other on the phone every morning while getting ready for school. "I think so, let me check. The one in the blue bottle, right? Shaped sort of like a teardrop?"

"That's the one. If you find it, can I borrow it again, please?"

More rustling. "Found it!" Rose yelled triumphantly. "I'll bring it with me. You really should buy your own though."

Lana laughed. "Thanks, girl. I owe you one." She

turned to Jade, who was sitting on her bed examining her nails. "You're right, I really should buy my own stuff. I'm always borrowing things from you guys," she shrugged. She hung up the phone and tossed it in her purse.

Jade looked up at her friend. "You know we don't mind," she smiled. "I don't know about you," she said as she went back to her nails, "but I just don't feel like going to school today. We should totally ditch." She said, tucking her feet underneath her.

"You know I would love to, but my parents would kill me," Lana answered, brushing out her long hair.

"I'm just so sick of Queen Veronica and her posse. You'd think they could let up on the teasing just once. Just one day I would like to be able to walk around school and not have to worry about rumors, or garbage being dumped on my head in the cafeteria, or dead animals being shoved in my locker." She shuddered at that last thought. The girls never retaliated in hopes that the torture would stop, but there was no stopping Veronica.

"I know what you mean," Lana sighed. "She's never been nice, but this year she kicked up the bitchiness a few notches."

Jade laughed.

"This is our senior year though," Lana continued. "Maybe she'll cool off soon. Or at least find someone else to pick on for a while."

"Doubt it. You know her, she's not happy until everyone around her is miserable. It's been that way since I've known her."

Lana drove both her friends to school, and they sat at their usual bench outside as they awaited the first morning bell.

"Do you guys have your costumes yet?" Rose asked, bouncing on her seat.

Jade took off her sunglasses to address her friend. "Don't you think we're a little too old to be dressing up?"

"You're never too old for Halloween," she shot back, looking slightly offended.

Lana just laughed as she laid in the sun, enjoying the unseasonable warmth.

"You freaks are too old for everything," a voice said.

Veronica stood before them with a sneer on her face. "And it's not like the three of you need a costume anyway. You're scary and freaky looking enough as it is." Her followers laughed.

The three of them stood there silently. They had

learned not to engage Veronica in any sort of conversation. It wasn't worth it, she would always win.

Veronica tossed her hair over her shoulder. "What's wrong? Black cat got your tongue?" She laughed again. She got down right in Lana's face. "The three of you will never be anything other than the nasty, disgusting freaks that you are. No one will ever accept you. No one will ever love you." She stared Lana in the eye, waiting for her to speak. But she bit her tongue and kept it all in.

Finally, she stood up. "I'm done with you. Freaks." She added as she walked away.

"Oh, I hate her so much," Jade fumed once she was out of earshot.

"Me too," Lana replied. "She needs to be taught a lesson. This has gone on long enough." She turned to her friends, eyes shining with ideas. "What do you say we meet up at the old house this weekend and come up with something extra special for her?"

"I like that idea," Rose smiled.

"Count me in," Jade said, throwing one more look in Veronica's direction. "It's about time someone took that bitch down."

FOUR

S aturday couldn't come soon enough. The girls had spent everyday after school researching spells, looking for the perfect one to take care of their little bully problem.

They went out to their favorite place to hang out: an old abandoned house in the middle of the woods. It was rundown and kind of smelly, but it suited their needs perfectly. No one ever bothered them there. No one else knew of its existence. It was so old that the forest had begun to reclaim it, and from the outside it just looked like an enormous mass of trees and moss at first glance. The girls had stumbled upon it by accident one night while wandering around the woods after having a little too much to drink.

After a while of them visiting with no interruptions they claimed it as their own. Out here there was no one to bully them, no one to tease them or call them freaks. They were free to just be themselves. Out here they were free to work on their witchcraft.

They had all stumbled into it early last summer, and were drawn to its seductive power. It's what drew them to each other, and the three of them have been inseparable ever since. Nothing could tear them apart.

Lana picked up the other two girls since she was the only one who had a car, and they headed out to their secret spot. You could practically feel the excitement in the air. They had been studying witchcraft since last year, but have yet to actually cast a spell. This would be their first time.

When they arrived Rose set out a fresh bowl of food and water by the front door for Spirit, the black cat that occasionally hung around the house.

"Why don't you just adopt the thing?" Jade asked her.

Rose let out a sigh. "You know I'd love to, but my dad is deathly allergic to cats."

"Or so he says."

"No, he really is," Rose replied with a nod. "I've been trying for years to get him to let me have a pet."

"Well, that's too bad then," shrugged Jade.

"Yeah, but having old Spirit here is good enough for me. I still get to take care of and love the little guy." Rose smiled and led the way into the house.

Lana located the Book of Shadows containing all their spells while Jade lit a few candles around the room. They had them stashed all over the house, both for use in spells and for light since there was no electricity running out here.

The Book of Shadows was something that Lana had found tucked away in her attic one day. She didn't know who it belonged to, just that it must have been someone in her family. On the cover was her family crest and her last name. But that was it, no first name or mention of anyone else's name found anywhere in the book. But every page was filled with spells, incantations, spell ingredients, and more. Every inch of the book was filled in with cramped handwriting, making most of it almost impossible to decipher.

Lana was sitting at home one day, bored, when she felt something calling to her from the attic. The call was so strong she just couldn't ignore it, so up she went, and snooped around until at last she located the book. She swore it just about vibrated at her touch, and she knew it was special. That it was what had been calling to her.

It cemented the feeling she had about her being meant to be a witch and to study witchcraft. She found comfort and meaning in the texts.

The three best friends practiced in secret and swore to never tell another soul about their newfound passion. No one would understand. And they were teased in life enough as it was.

Each girl had their own personal, yet similar experiences that led them to believing in witchcraft and that it was what they were meant to do.

That it was a part of them, of who they were.

Rose had been upset one day after being turned down yet about getting a family pet. She was always so gentle and nurturing. She just wanted a little puppy or kitty of her very own to love and always be there for her. Rose hated being alone, and longed for a little furry companion. That night at dinner she was still upset. She sat down at the table but refused to speak to her parents. She was through arguing and didn't want to cry in front of them.

Her parents tried only once to engage her in conversation before shrugging their shoulders and then simply ignoring her. As her mother made last minute preparations and began bringing the food to the table, her anger began to build. She hated feeling this way and closed her eyes to try and steady her emotions.

Instead she took two deep breaths and then her eyes flew back open at the sound of her mother screaming in pain. The pot of mashed potatoes had somehow exploded right in her face as she carried it to the table. It wasn't on the heat on the stove or anything. Her mother dropped what remained of the pot as she was struck with scolding potatoes and metal shards from the pot.

Rose sat there stunned as her father jumped up to help her mother. She couldn't hear a word her father said, her mother's screams faded away. She just felt guilt, and shame. Since that incident she has worked harder to control her emotions. Rose never had any fits of anger after that and as a result, no more incidents.

Jade was out getting her hair done when hers happened. She arrived early to her appointment and after checking in, sat in the waiting room with a magazine. She could hear laughter coming from the two girls sitting across from her. She tried to ignore it but they just got louder and louder as if trying to get her attention. When Jade finally looked up from the article she was reading the two girls stopped staring at her, and almost fell off their chairs and they laughed even harder.

As she rolled her eyes her name was called. Breathing a sigh of relief she walked past the two girls and sat in the stylists chair. She had just finished trimming the back of her hair when one of the girls who was laughing at her took the seat next to her.

Jade fumed as the girl stared at her through the mirror with a taunting expression on her face. The stylist moved to work on Jade's bangs and she was glad not to be able to see her anymore.

Then the laughter resumed. Jade bit her lip, trying not to let it bother her. But she could feel the anger boiling inside her. She sniffed the air, smelling something odd.

Just then screams from the chair next to her. Jade whipped her head around to see the commotion, almost getting cut in the eye in the process.

Her mouth fell open at the sight of the girl with her hair on fire. The straightener that was being used on her now laid on the floor, melted and mangled.

There's no way I caused that, was Jade's first

thought. She shook her head, knowing damn well she can't control things like that to happen.

But it would be awesome if she could.

That thought stayed with her for weeks after her appointment, and she noticed similar things would happen when someone would piss her off enough. Something bad would always happen, even if she didn't directly wish for it to happen. That was enough for her to believe.

Lana's love of magic began earlier than the other two. She had learned a couple years ago that she may have some sort of ability, when she found she was able to move objects with her mind, not far, but still able to move them, and she too could make things explode or catch fire or something when her emotions were strong enough.

Lana kept her abilities a secret, but she still practiced them whenever she could.

"Okay, girls," Lana said as she stopped on a page about a third of the way through the book. "I think this is the one. This is the spell that will help us out with Veronica. Jade, did you manage to get a lock of her hair?" She asked as Rose bent over to check out the spell.

Jade rummaged around in her bag. "I did, and it was a disgusting job. Please don't make me do anything like that ever again," she replied, holding up a plastic bag containing some of Veronica's hair. "She left her brush lying around in the locker room after gym the other day. Made it all too easy for me. Here, take this," she handed Lana the bag. She set it down next to a large candle.

"Hopefully this is all we'll need," she said.

"You're not sure?" Rose asked, looking up from the pages she was reading.

Lana shifted uncomfortably. "Well, I"ve never actually attempted anything like this before," she admitted. "But neither have the two of you," she quickly added, making sure she wouldn't be the only one to blame in case something went wrong.

"True."

Jade clapped her hands and rubbed them together. "So let's get this started. I'm ready."

The girls gathered around the candle. Lana placed the book in the center, so that they could all read it. Placing their left hand on the shoulder of the person next to them, they connected their little circle. In their free hand they each held a piece of Veronica's hair.

Softly at first, they began to chant. As they continued their voices grew louder and the pace quickened.

"Place the hair in the fire," Lana instructed. As they laid it in the flame she closed her eyes, saying Veronica's name over and over and chanting something in a language neither Rose nor Jade knew. They threw each other a quick glance but remained silent, letting Lana finish. As she spoke the room began to fill with a light fog, the flames dancing wildly on all the candles in the room. They cast eerie shadows all around.

As Lana uttered the last syllable her eyes flew open, and at once the flames stopped their dance and the fog disappeared.

"Whoa," Rose breathed.

"Yeah," Jade added. "You think it worked?" She asked in a whisper.

Lana closed the book. "Well, we'll have to wait until Monday when we see her at school, but I've got a good feeling about it," she smiled, hugging the book close to her chest.

FIVE

The girls arrived extra early to school on Monday, eager to see if their spell had worked or not.

"Jade, will you stop moving and fidgeting around so much?" Lana asked, a little impatient.

Jade never sat still when she was nervous. She was always all over the place. Rose was the same way, but when she was excited, not nervous.

"I'm sorry, I can't help it," she admitted. "I just want to know if it worked or not already."

"Well, we're about to get our chance," Lana pointed. "Because here she comes."

They all looked as Veronica pulled her car into a parking space and hopped out. She greeted her friends and then they walked right up to the front of the building.

"You freaks really should be kept hidden behind the school. You make the rest of us look bad," she laughed as she walked into the school.

"Not even a scratch on her. Still has perfect hair, teeth, and body," Jade said in a mocking tone. "What happened?" She asked, turning to Lana.

She shook head as she grabbed her backpack. "I'm not sure. I guess it didn't work."

"Well, that sucks," Rose added.

"Sure does, " Jade replied. "It's not fair, nothing bad ever happens to her.

And nothing bad did happen until about halfway through the school day. The girls were in English class, when suddenly their teacher stopped writing on the blackboard and fainted, hitting her head on the sharp corner of her desk. The class panicked and a few others screamed as someone ran to get both the principal and nurse.

Jade, Lana, and Rose just looked at each other with terrified looks on their faces. Mrs Cooper was a favorite teacher of theirs. She had always treated the three of them with respect, and not at all like they were different, or freaks.

The principal got on the intercom and announced to the entire school that class was dismissed for the rest of the day.

Mrs Cooper had died.

SIX

"God, I never thought they would let us go." Jade said as they walked out the front doors of the school. Parents with worried looks on their faces crowded the front of the building, waiting to pick up their kids.

Lana pointed to a woman running through the crowd. "Hey Rose," she said, bumping her friend on the shoulder. "Isn't that your mom?" It was strange to see her mom there, she never picked Rose up from school. Lana had always given her a ride.

Rose never got a chance to answer. Her mother quickly spotted her and ran faster, tackling her daughter in a hug. "You're all right!" She exclaimed, checking Rose over for any scrapes or bruises or anything else that might be wrong with her.

"Yeah, mom. I'm fine." Rose wiggled out of her mother's grasp.

"What a freak." Veronica laughed as she walked by. Jade glared at her.

Rose's mother tugged on her arm. "Come on, we have to go. Now." It sounded urgent.

"Slow down, mom. I'm okay. And you're starting to worry me."

Her mother turned and looked Rose straight in the face, eyes shining with tears. "But your brother's not," she said tearfully. "I got another call right before I got the one from your school. It was his coach. He's had some sort of football accident. It's pretty bad, and he's in the hospital."

The three girls looked at each other with terrified looks on their faces. Rose's brother, Tyler was a huge football star. The best at school, he always had scouts after him. He never had any accidents or injuries while playing. In fact, he was usually the one to give the other players the injury.

This was really bad.

Face pale, Rose silently nodded and followed her mother to the car. They drove off to the hospital so fast they nearly had an accident themselves.

"You don't think . . ." Jade whispered once they were gone.

Lana shook her head slowly. "Of course not. There's no way we could have possibly caused all this." She didn't sound too confident at all. "Besides, we directed the . . ." she lowered her voice, glancing around to make sure no one was listening in on their conversation, "spell at Veronica. So if anything were to happen as a result of what we did, she should be the one affected. The only one. But look." she said, pointing to their enemy, who was laughing obnoxiously, tossing her long blonde hair over her shoulder and flirting with any guy that would listen to her. Which was pretty much every guy with a pulse.

"I know," Jade huffed. "Nothing happened to her. Not even something as small as tripping in the hallway." She let out a small laugh. "I would have loved to see that."

"I would have too, but focus," Lana said sternly.

Jade shut right up. "Sorry."

Lana waved off her apology. "We have to figure out what's happening. And fast."

Jade nodded. "Agreed."

"So what do you say we sneak out tonight, read over the spell we used. See if we can figure out where everything went wrong?"

"No," Jade said, shaking her head. "I don't want to go home right now. What if something terrible happened right at my house? I couldn't face it, especially not if we were the cause of it." She wrapped her arms tightly around herself.

"All right, we can go now. Come on," she said, leading her friend through the mess of people still standing around outside of the school.

Veronica happened to be standing near Lana's car, so they had no choice but to walk by her.

"Where do you think you're going, freaks?" She sure loved to use that word, especially when referring to them. "Don't you think we all know that the three of you are responsible for this mess? I mean, who else could it possibly be?"

Jade opened her mouth to respond but Lana pulled her away and into the car. "We really don't want to start anything right now," she whispered, trying her best to ignore the laughter and accusing stares all around them.

Jade stared daggers at Veronica until they drove out of sight, wishing she would just burst into flames or something. "I really wish that the spell had worked on her," she complained. She sat back in her seat and folded her arms across her chest.

Lana chuckled. Me too, she thought. Me too.

She drove to the abandoned house as fast as she could, anxious to figure out this whole mess. She swore she did everything right.

It would have been a huge help to have Rose with them, but she understood why she wasn't. She had to be at the hospital with her brother. He would need her.

When they arrived near the house, Lana parked in her usual spot, hidden under a few bent tree branches. They quickly unbuckled their seatbelts and took off towards the front door.

"I'll check the Book of Shadows," Lana said, ducking to miss a low hanging branch.

"Great. And I'll, uh . . ."

"You can be in charge of the phones," Lana offered. "Maybe keep an eye out for any messages, any more emergencies."

Jade nodded. "Got it."

They hurried through the door, Lana tossing her phone to Jade as she went straight for the book. Even though no one dared to ever visit the house she still preferred to keep it hidden. You can never be too careful.

Jade set the ringers on high volume to make sure she didn't miss any incoming call or message, and sat down on the floor. She gently placed the phones in front of her and sat, with her head in her hands, staring at the blank screens. She willed them to stay silent, not sure she could take any more bad news.

Lana located the book and quickly flipped to the page containing the spell they used. She read the whole thing over twice, thinking back to what happened when they cast it. She was sure they pronounced everything correctly, didn't miss or add any unnecessary words. She shook her head, frustrated and confused.

"I don't know!" She yelled in frustration, startling Jade. "I don't know what went wrong. I can't find anything."

"Maybe it wasn't us then?" Jade offered, shrugging her shoulders. "We can't be the only witches in town. We've been keeping it a secret, so there really is no way of knowing if they are too."

Lana looked back down at the opened pages. When she had yelled out she pushed the book away from her a bit, and it now laid at an angle. She squinted, there was some small writing that she hadn't noticed before.

Her hand flew to her mouth. Lana slowly looked up to her friend, eyes wide. "It was us," she said in a small shaky voice.

Jade stood. "How do you know?" She asked slowly, not sure if she wanted to know or not based on her friend's expression.

Lana didn't answer, just pointed to the passage she just discovered.

Jade bent down to see what had freaked Lana out so bad. She located the words, and read out loud.

"BEWARE THIS SPELL.

    For it brings darkness not light.

    If you are not skilled

    In the art of magic

    You will invite

    Death into your life.

    Beware this spell."

"BUT WHAT DOES IT MEAN?" Jade asked. "It doesn't make sense to me.".

Lana took the book from her. "I'm not entirely sure, but I think it's some kind of warning. That this spell isn't what we thought it was. That it will do more harm than good."

Jade threw her hands up in the air. "So,

what...are you saying we just invited death into our world. That it's after us instead of merely playing a trick on Veronica."

Lana looked up at her friend, fear in her eyes. "Basically."

CHAPTER
SEVEN

"Oh, my god," Jade said, pacing back and forth. "What are we going to do? This is serious." She turned to Lana, still poring through the Book of Shadows, trying to find a solution, some way to maybe reverse the spell they cast.

Spells can be reversed, right?

"I don't know," Lana answered, flipping furiously through the pages. "There has to be something though. Something else we missed."

"Like what?" Jade yelled, her voice echoing off the walls. Desperation filled her voice. "We already missed the warning, what more could there possibly be?"

"Like I said, I don't know," Lana replied, trying

to keep her own voice calm. "But I'm going to find it."

"Well hurry, please."

Lana eyed her friend. She knew Jade didn't mean to be so bossy. She was stressed. They all were. She shook her head and set back to searching for the hidden answer she was sure had to be there.

Jade got tired of pacing and took to wandering the rest of the house, leaving Lana to read in peace.

After what felt like hours of searching, Lana closed her eyes and rubbed them gently, giving them a break from the strain of staring at the pages. When she opened them again she noticed the room was filled with a thick, black colored smoke. Lana blinked a few times, thinking she was just seeing things in her exhausted state.

But the smoke remained.

"Jade?" She called out. "Jade, you're not smoking again, are you? Or knocking over any candles?" She didn't smoke all that often, but the last time she did Jade almost set the whole place on fire. It didn't help that the abandoned house was filled with leaves and twigs, and made from old rotting wood.

"Jade?" She called a third time, with a little more urgency.

Still no answer.

Lana was starting to really worry. With each minute that passed the smoke grew thicker, filling half the room by now. If there really was a fire she needed to find Jade and get the hell out of here.

As she looked around she noticed the doorway was completely blocked by the smoke. It was the only way out of the room.

Crap.

Lana sucked in a deep breath, and shielding her eyes with her arm, ran towards the door. Her skin began to burn wherever the smoke came in contact with her. She opened her mouth to scream, and the smoke quickly filled her lungs, burning the entire way down.

Choking, tears stinging her eyes, Lana fell to her knees. The air near the floor was mostly clear, but it hardly gave her any relief. Through the pain, she was still determined to find her friend. Clawing her way across the floor, she found herself at the bottom of the stairs. The last time she remembered seeing Jade was when she gave up her pacing and walked up the stairs to the second floor to wander around. Jade never could stay still when she was nervous or anxious.

Lana closed her eyes again and began to drag herself slowly up the stairs. Along with the

34

burning sensation her energy was being drained, fast.

She kept pulling herself up until she ran into an obstacle. Eyes still closed due to the amount of smoke, she felt around with her hands to see if she could move and maybe identify the object in her way. Whatever it was felt soft, yet heavy.

Prying her eyes open a sliver, she realized the smoke was just too thick to see anything, so she quickly snapped them shut again. She had no choice but to try and crawl over top of it.

As she began to pull herself over the obstacle in front of her, she stopped short when she felt something familiar-hair. Human hair.

Screams ripped from her raw, burned throat as she realized she had been trying to climb over the body of her best friend. Lana frantically felt around, trying to find a pulse on Jade or some sign that she was still breathing.

Nothing.

She slumped back against the railing in defeat. She didn't know what to do. She didn't know where she was anymore, let alone how to get out of here. The smoke had scrambled her brain.

If she could, Lana would cry. But her insides felt like ash.

"Lana! Jade! Where is everyone?" Rose coughed. She had never been so glad to hear Rose's voice in her life.

When she opened her mouth to yell out to her friend, nothing came out. So she tried banging on the railing to get Rose's attention.

"Guys! Where are you? What is all this smoke? Is everyone all right?"

Her voice was getting louder, which was a good sign. It meant Rose was getting closer and she would soon be rescued. Lana slid down the stairs towards Rose's voice.

"Oh, my god!" Rose screamed. "What the hell happened to you Lana?" She asked as her friend appeared. Lana had been in the smoke so long that the skin on her face had nearly melted right off.

Rose gagged.

"Where is Jade?" She asked in a panicked voice.

Without saying a word Lana pointed up the stairs. Rose took off her sweater and covered her face with it, hoping to protect herself as she went off in search of her friend.

She didn't know if she could help. But she couldn't. Nothing could. Once you spoke those words, unleashed that dark magic, nothing could help you.

It wouldn't stop until you and everyone you ever loved was dead.

The smoke, having done its job, cleared right up, leaving no trace of its existence.

No one ever did manage to find those three best friends, as they remained a charred, melted mess of skin and bones down the stairs of that abandoned house.

Let this be a warning to anyone wanting to dabble in dark magic. It is not kind, it will not do your bidding. You mess with it, and it will mess with you right back.

And will not stop until all is dead.

FLAMES OF REVENGE

J.M. Goodrich

FLAMES OF REVENGE

Every morning since he had met Tayliss, Troy woke up feeling like he was on top of the world. Only today was extra special because it was their one year anniversary. Normally, he wouldn't get excited about this kind of thing, but Troy had completely fallen head over heels for this woman.

To celebrate the occasion they had both taken the day off. "Happy anniversary," he whispered, gently kissing her behind the ear.

"Are you ready for your surprise?" She asked as she slid her arms around him.

He planted a kiss on her forehead. "You know it."

They got into the car and drove out to the middle of the woods, where Tayliss had suggested they have their celebration.

As they reached their destination, she handed Troy a blindfold and asked him to put it on.

Troy laughed and slipped on the blindfold, his excitement building. He waited while Tayliss came around to his side to help guide him out. "Do you trust me?" She whispered, her lips grazing his cheek.

Troy shivered at her touch. "With my life."

"Take my hands. We don't have far to go." She led him a little ways into the woods, still not giving him any hints.

"We're here!" She announced at last. She stopped Troy as he began to remove his blindfold. "Not yet," she told him in a seductive voice.

"Lay down," she instructed him, and he obeyed. Around each of his arms and legs she tied a rope, which were also connected to nearby trees.

Kinky, he thought, his excitement building even more.

"It's time," she said as she removed Troy's blindfold. He blinked until his vision came back into focus. He found himself lying in a dirt pit that was surrounded by candles.

And a shovel.

No pillows, blankets. No wine. Nothing romantic.

"What's going on?" he asked, trying to keep any accusation out of his voice.

"You really don't know, do you?" She asked, venom seeping into her voice.

"I don't," Troy admitted, tugging on the ropes that held him captive. "Let me go, please."

"I'm afraid I can't do that," she said, picking up a bottle as she continued, "You really don't recognize me? Here, get a good look," she said, getting directly in his face.

"What is this? You're crazy!"

"Who . . . am I?" She asked again.

"Tayliss, you're Tayliss," he answered quickly.

Her laughter echoed off the trees. "Not exactly. The first part of my name is right, though."

"What the hell are you talking about?"

She didn't answer him, she just opened up the bottle she was holding and began pouring the contents in a circle around Troy, dumping some directly on him as well.

The smell hit him - lighter fluid. "What the hell is this?" He demanded.

"Do you remember what happened about two years ago now?" Tayliss asked, ignoring his question. "Remember what you did?" The bottle now empty, she hopped up out of the pit, continuing to circle him on higher ground.

He didn't like this game.

"Aww, you look lost. Let me help ," she said, stopping close to Troy's face so he could see her better. "About two years ago now, you decided that you didn't want a wife anymore. Or at least, the one you had. Do you remember what you did? Something similar to this, huh?" She gestured to their surroundings.

Troy's eyes grew wide. "T-Taylor?" he asked, his voice shaky. "How do you know about that? How do you know about her?" He demanded, his voice barely above a whisper .No one was supposed to know about that,

He was careful.

Taylor was dead.

Tayliss threw her head back and laughed. "I don't know her, silly. I am her."

"Impossible," he spat. "She's gone. My wife died years ago." He had made sure of that.

"No, dear," she said as she stroked his cheek, "you only thought that I died." Sighing, she stood back up and hopped out of the pit. "I spent months getting my body fixed, the scars erased. At least the scars on the outside".

"Why are you doing this?"

Taylor glared at him. "You can't be serious! Revenge! What else? I was nothing but a loyal, loving wife to you and what did you do? You beat me unconscious, dragged me out to the middle of nowhere, and left me to burn to death." She quickly turned away, not wanting him to see the tears forming.

"I never could figure out why you did it." She added.

Troy remained silent.

"Well," Taylor said, wiping her face, "I'm not going to make the same mistake."

"Taylor, please! We can. . . we can work this out. I'll tell you anything you want to know." Troy panicked. "We just had the most amazing year together, haven't we?" he asked, trying anything to get her to release him. "I'm sorry, Taylor. I love you. I see now how amazing you are and how perfect we are together. Untie me and we can start over. We can be us again."

Despite his pleas, she began kicking each candle one by one into the pit, not stopping until every one had contributed to her morbid bonfire.

Taylor watched as the man who was once her husband, her lover slowly burned to a crisp. She knew she should feel something as she watched his skin melt off his bones and drip to the dirt. But she felt nothing.

Once the smoke cleared and she was satisfied that he was really, truly dead, she picked up her shovel and began to fill in Troy's makeshift grave, making sure to pack in his mouth and nose real tight, blocking all airways.

The dirt now smoothed over and covered with random rocks, leaves, and twigs, Taylor made one more sweep of the area to make sure she hadn't left anything behind. She didn't want a single thing to tie her to this.

She breathed a heavy sigh of relief and headed back to the car, eager to finally be able to move on with her life.

As Taylor.